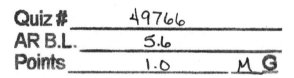

Quiz #   49766
AR B.L.   5.6
Points   1.0   M G

A BOOK OF
COUPONS

by Susie Morgenstern
illustrated by Serge Bloch
translated by Gill Rosner

VIKING

VIKING

Published by the Penguin Group

Penguin Putnam Books for Young Readers,

345 Hudson Street, New York, New York 10014, U.S.A.

Penguin Books Ltd, Registered Offices: Harmondsworth, Middlesex, England

First published in France in 1999 by l'école des loisirs, under the title *Joker*.
Published in the United States of America in 2001 by Viking,
a division of Penguin Putnam Books for Young Readers.

10 9 8 7 6 5 4 3 2 1

LIBRARY OF CONGRESS CATALOGING-IN-PUBLICATION DATA
Morgenstern, Susie Hoch.
A book of coupons / by Susie Morgenstern ; illustrated by Serge Bloch.
    p.   cm.
Summary: Elderly Monsieur Noël, the very unconventional new fifth-grade
teacher, gives coupon books for such things as dancing in class and
sleeping late, which are bound to get him in trouble with the military
discipline of Principal Incarnation Perez.
ISBN 0-670-89970-4 (hardcover)
[1. Teachers—Fiction. 2. Schools—Fiction. 3. Humorous stories.]
I. Bloch, Serge, ill. II. Title.
PZ7.M826714 Bo 2001   [Fic]—dc21   00–011940

Printed in U.S.A.
Set in Stempel Schneidler and Greymantle
Book design by Teresa Kietlinski

For David Hercky ... who knows all about

the right coupons for life

A BOOK OF
COUPONS

to be honest, all the kids were happy to be going back to school. The lazy French summer was on its way out, and boredom had begun to creep into those long hot afternoons. That's why everyone was secretly looking forward to the new year. So, in spite of their grumbling and complaining, deep down they couldn't wait; and even if they were a little bit nervous about meeting their new teacher, it was, all things considered, high time for this final year of elementary school to begin.

It must be said that the teacher they found when they walked into their classroom on that first day was the last one they expected. There he was, sitting behind his desk like some unmovable tree trunk. Charles wondered how it was possible that a *new* teacher could be so incredibly *old*. Mohammed peered more closely at the enormous man to make sure he wasn't seeing double . . . or triple. Could all those wrinkles be real? They all looked at each other apprehensively. They were completely, utterly, and inescapably disappointed. They had been hoping for a young teacher who was athletic and handsome, but they had been given a fat old man who looked like those pictures of God, with messy white hair and reading glasses perched on the end of his nose, not to mention the balloon of a potbelly—which was probably the nearest they would get to anything resembling a ball this year. In their school, there was no special gym teacher. Each teacher decided when, or when *not*, to have gym, and this teacher really didn't seem like the gung-ho gym type.

And they were just as shocked by the sound of his voice. It made Nina jump to hear the deep bass growl which sounded like something from the bowels of the earth. They were surprised by his first words, which were not *Good morning,*

not *My name is* . . . not even *Sit down please,* but simply "I have a present for you." And with that, this monstrosity who was to serve as their teacher deposited a gift-wrapped package on each student's desk.

Was this a peace offering? An apology for his age and appearance? Whatever it was, he didn't so much as glance at any of them while he was handing them out.

Constance tore her present open and found a book of coupons. An ordinary book of coupons, like a book of raffle tickets sold for charity. A book of coupons with dotted lines along the edge of the pages where you tore them off. Everyone got one.

"Don't tell me we're going to spend the year tearing out coupons!" cried Benedicte, thinking of her grandpa in America, who spent his life sticking Green Stamps in a book. Once he filled the book, he could trade it in for a silver-plated tray or a set of dishes. But then she was the first to realize that these were not just ordinary store coupons or even Green Stamps. It was a pack of vouchers. Every single voucher in the book had "One coupon" written on it. Below that was a description. The teacher tapped on Charles's desk to ask him to read out what was written on his coupons. Charles wondered if this teacher happened to be some kind of visitor from prehistoric times, as all he could do was point and grunt instead of speaking normally. However, he obeyed the silent request, and his initial surprise turned into utter astonishment as he started reading out loud:

One coupon for sleeping late
One coupon for skipping a day of school
One coupon for being late to school
One coupon for losing your homework
One coupon for forgetting your books
One coupon for not listening in class

One coupon for sleeping in class
One coupon for copying from your neighbor
One coupon for not going when
    called to the blackboard
One coupon for getting out of trouble
One coupon for eating in class
One coupon for making a lot of noise

Charles couldn't believe his eyes. The teacher
pointed at Benedicte to continue.

One coupon for singing at the top of your lungs
    wherever you like
One coupon for dancing in class
One coupon for taking a break from class
One coupon for clowning around
One coupon for telling a lie
One coupon for giving the teacher a kiss on the cheek

At this point, Benedicte could go no further. The teacher signaled to Mohammed that it was his turn.

One coupon for hugging whomever you like
One coupon for taking your own sweet time
One coupon for a never-ending recess
One coupon for forgetting the books for
    your assignment
One coupon for a longer vacation
The *wild card* coupon

While the list was being read, the kids were puzzled and excited, but since it was still the first day of school, it was far too early to get noisy about it. And then, out of the blue, the booming voice spoke out. "My name is Hubert Noël. Ever since I was young, and I assure you that once upon a time I *was* young, people have called me Santa. That is why I became a teacher—I love giving presents, and I am going to give them to you every single day. I'm giving you the whole year of lessons for free. I'm giving away books. I'm giving away penmanship and spelling. I'm giving away math and science. I'm giving away everything life has taught me. I'm even throwing in the cataclysms."

"What does 'cataclysm' mean?" asked Constance.

"Well," he replied, picking up the dictionary, "here's another magical gift. In this book you have, in order, the meaning of every word." He handed Constance the dictionary, open at the letter C. She saw what he wanted her to read: "Cataclysm: a sudden and violent disaster or disturbance such as a flood, earthquake, or tornado." Only Charles was close enough to the teacher to hear his sad whisper:

"Or the death of a loved one."

"Use this word three times, and it will be yours—a present from me and the dictionary to you!"

Charles was not fooled by Monsieur Noël's

enthusiasm. He knew that 'cataclysm' was not a word you could use every day.

"You can put away your coupons, class. Use them whenever you need to from now on. Now I've got another present for you."

He gave out another gift-wrapped package. Opening their gifts, the kids realized that they had all been given the same book: *David Copperfield* by Charles Dickens. It was a thick book written in small, closely set print without

a single illustration. It was definitely not a tempting book; in fact it was quite the opposite.

"But Monsieur, this isn't a real present. Look, it's got 'School Property' stamped inside," said Charles.

But that didn't bother Santa. "Even if this book does not legally belong to you, it is yours from the moment that you read it. My gift to you is the story, the characters, the words, the ideas, the style, the emotions. Once you have read the book, all these things will be yours for life. I'll start by reading it to you, and you can finish it for the end of the week."

"Impossible!" Benedicte couldn't help shouting. She set off a revolt that was almost the French Revolution. Everyone started hunting frantically for a "coupon for not reading a book," but in vain. The teacher didn't notice. He started reading in a voice that sounded like a Shakespearean actor:

Whether I shall turn out to be the hero of my own life, or whether that station will be held by anybody else, these pages must show. To begin my life with the beginning of my life, I record that I was born (as I have been informed and believe) on a Friday, at twelve o'clock at night. It was remarked that the clock began to strike, and I began to cry, simultaneously. In consideration of the day and hour of my birth, it was declared by the nurse, and by some sage women in the neighbourhood who had taken a lively interest in me several months before there was any possibility of our becoming personally acquainted, first, that I was destined to be unlucky in life; and secondly, that I was privileged to see ghosts and spirits; both these gifts inevitably attaching, as they believed, to all unlucky infants of either gender, born towards the small hours on a Friday night.

They listened carefully. After all, the more the teacher read, the less *they* would have to read by themselves.

By the time lunch came, the kids in the class didn't know what to think. Sure, they loved the coupons, but this teacher was just too weird. He didn't walk with them to the cafeteria, as if by sparing himself the exercise, he could save his energy.

"We can forget about gym!" said Laurent bitterly, feeling sure that this Monsieur Muscles was never going to want to play ball with them.

But at the end of the meal, the teacher did show up at the cafeteria, with yet another present for each kid—a toothbrush and a miniature tube of toothpaste. He led them to the bathroom to make sure that they used them according to his directions. "Your teeth are precious jewels. Make sure you brush them."

Charles was the first to make use of a coupon.

In the middle of the math lesson, he broke out singing: "Frère Jacques, Frère Jacques. Dormez-vous? Dormez-vous?" The teacher collected his coupon and stopped the lesson. Then he handed out a songsheet with the words to the French national anthem and announced, "Okay, now we're all going to sing!

"*Allons enfants de la patrie*
Le jour de gloire est arrivé."

"But Monsieur Noël," wailed Serge, "we don't get what this song is talking about!"

"You don't have to understand. How does it make you feel when you sing it?"

That night Charles stayed up past midnight reading *David Copperfield*. He couldn't put it down. The author was even named Charles, like him. Maybe Monsieur Noël was planning to invite Monsieur Dickens to come to school and talk to them, like the writers who had been invited to come in and talk to the kids last year.

In the morning, Charles was too tired to get up. "I don't have to go yet. I've got a coupon."

"A coupon?"

"Yes, just look in my book bag and you'll see it." Charles was too tired to get up and fish it out himself.

"Is this what you mean?" His mother showed him the book of coupons. Charles pushed his pillow away from his face and nodded yes.

His mother didn't believe him at first, but here it was right in her hand: "One coupon for sleeping late." What could she do but give in?

By half past ten he had gotten bored and he wanted to go to school. He handed in his coupon as he entered the classroom, but once it was in the teacher's hand, he suddenly felt sad that he didn't have it anymore. He whispered to Sylvie, "I'll give you anything you want if you'll give me your coupon for skipping a day of school."

"Okay, you can have it in exchange for three other coupons."

That week, aside from Charles's, eight coupons were used: Benedicte for eating in class, Mohammed for not going up to the blackboard, Constance for losing your homework, and five others for being late for school.

At the end of yet another weird week, Laurent announced, "He should have given us a coupon for going to gym."

"I'd have liked a coupon for bringing your dog to school," said Charles. He had already used up nearly all his coupons, unlike Sylvie, who was collecting more and more of them, thanks to the black market that had begun during recess.

As for Laurent, he had stashed his coupons away carefully in his schoolbag. He was dying to use one. So he took them out, picked one at random, and then just stood there staring at it. When Charles, peeking over his shoulder, dared him to use it right then and there, Laurent thought, "Why not!" He began dancing around frantically, right in the middle of history class. (Maybe this way he would make history himself.)

When the teacher took the coupon from Laurent, he had a wonderful inspiration! Suddenly he was moving the tables out of the way.

"Hey kids, gather round. I'm going to teach you a dance I used to do when I was your age. It's called the jitterbug." And with that, he turned on the CD player full blast, and alone in the middle of the room, started whirling around like a dervish.

It was probably not the best time for the principal to pay an unexpected visit. However, the would-be Broadway star didn't seem unhappy to see her. She was just the dancing partner he was looking for. He took her hand

and led her, much against her will, into the swing of things.

But she would have nothing to do with his Broadway revival and pushed him away with such vehemence that she sent the fat teacher spinning against the tables, his glasses falling to the floor and his trouser button flying into the air.

"The principal is a cataclysm!" cried Constance, delighted at finally being able to put her word to use.

"I want to see you in my office this afternoon," said the principal to Monsieur Noël.

The principal, Madame Incarnation Perez, had been loved by nobody except for her husband, and *he* had escaped relatively lightly . . . by dying. She lived in the apartment which came with the school, all alone, with no children and no pets. No one had ever seen her go out during the weekends. Whatever she did from morning to night between her own four walls remained a mystery. Maybe she spent her time looking for new ways to spread terror. She was universally hated, universally that is except for poor old Monsieur Noël, who although too old in one way, was too new in another. He had not yet had time to get to know Madame Perez, nor to hear the other teachers' stories.

In a word, Incarnation Perez was nuts. Sure, she may have had her reasons, but nevertheless she subjected the teachers and students of Marie Curie School to military discipline. Everyone knew that disobedience was suicidal.

But you see, just about nothing frightened Hubert Noël, certainly not Incarnation Pérez. His long experience as a teacher and as a human being had taught him that life just isn't that serious. After all, what could this woman do to him? He had nothing to lose. The only things that frightened him were abstract ideas like hatred. But he always set his sights on better things, like love. As for Incarnation Perez, she may have been close to sixty, but actually she was still rather nice looking if you asked him. He was glad that he had remembered to bring her a decent bottle of wine as an introduction. He knocked at her door and went in.

She didn't ask him to sit down. It was 4:45 in the afternoon. She sat there, and in her dry monotonous voice, she read to him out loud from the rule book with the statutes of the

school, and she read him the Civil Code on labor laws: "All employees must adhere to the laws and statutes of the institution, in strict obedience to the dress, behavior, and disciplinary code, under the authority of the head of the establishment and under penalty of punishment by article 6832 of penal law."

He couldn't get a word in. In fact, he wasn't even listening. Standing up tired him out. When she had finished, she got up and opened the door to throw him out. He left, with the bottle of wine still in his hand. He knew one thing—he didn't want to go back into that office again in this life or the next. He went home and plopped himself down into the first chair he saw, and drank the whole bottle himself.

Once a week, Monsieur Noël would take the children on a field trip. They had already done three months' worth, including trips to the supermarket, to the hospital, to the police station, and to City Hall. Like all the previous ones, today's trip was part of what Monsieur Noël called a lesson in "life's little trials." Today's trial was called "At the Post Office: Sending a Letter." Since Christmas was approaching, no one had any trouble coming up with destinations for a card or package. They were impressed by the enormous building that was the town's main post office, and the vast waiting area with its rows of hard chairs screwed to the floor. Monsieur Noël pointed out the little box on the wall that dispensed numbers. Each child took one. There were so many people already waiting that, despite the large number of chairs, they could not sit down. So each of them stood there waiting, eyes glued to the screen which would display their numbers in order. But what was taking so long? Hanging around with nowhere to go was a recipe for deadly boredom.

The first to crack was Mohammed, who broke into a hit song in Arabic. His coupons went everywhere with him. Constance tried out a belly dance. People stared at them as if they had escaped from the zoo.

At last, when all their numbers had been called, Monsieur Noël said, "See how hard it is to wait your turn? You need a lot of patience in life." The following week, he planned to take them to the train station so they could try their hand at buying train tickets from the automatic ticket machine. Once they had it right they would just push the button that said cancel.

⊘⊘

Poor Incarnation Perez! She didn't need the post office or the train station. There was nobody to send cards or packages to, and no one to take a train ride to see. On certain particularly unbearable Sundays in her orderly little apartment right next to the school, Incarnation Perez would wonder whether she was alive or dead. Sometimes, she really felt like she was wandering around in her own tomb. She could have called someone, but she had no one to call.

She could have cleaned the house, but it was already spotless. One way or another the weekdays went by, but weekends were dreadful. On the last day before Christmas vacation she watched Hubert Noël leave the school with his beaten-up old leather briefcase and his long coat with the hem dragging on the ground. He was the last straw.

Hubert Noël also managed to survive during the week, but holidays had become hard for him ever since he lost his wife. His children and grandchildren lived in other parts of the country, and even in other countries, so it was mostly on holidays that he managed to see them. He got busy before Christmas buying gifts for his four children and eleven grandchildren. And when he got on the train to visit them way up north, he looked more perfect than ever for the role of Santa. (He could have used a few reindeer to help with all his boxes and bags.)

Seeing his children always gave him a boost. Each of them made him proud and happy. They called and wrote to each other often, and had wanted him to buy a computer so that they could e-mail each other. But Hubert didn't take to the idea. Well, it didn't matter, because they went and bought him one for Christmas

Welcome to the 21st century

anyway! The card said "Welcome to the 21st century!" Now he would be as loaded up when he went back home as he had been when he came. The vacation was swallowed up with delicious meals and computer lessons. Christmas was the time he missed his wife most, so the hole in his heart was always there. But it seemed smaller with all the hugs and affection from all of his children.

It was only on the train back that, suddenly, Incarnation Perez came to mind. She hadn't bothered him since the last time he was in her office. In fact, they had avoided each other. Certainly a few parents found his teaching method somewhat bizarre, and even worried that their children might not learn enough to pass into junior high, but they were too intelligent to go and complain to this dragon of a principal.

When everyone was back in school after Christmas and New Year's, Monsieur Noël noticed that use of the coupons had almost completely died down. Too much, in fact, for his liking. The students didn't need the "coupon for not listening in class," because the classes were too interesting. They didn't need the "coupon for skipping a day of school," because they wanted to come too much.

Monsieur Noël reminded them, "Don't forget—you all have coupons in life. Any you don't use will die when you do." So at recess, the whole class discussed what Monsieur Noël had said, and they decided to take his advice. They all planned to use the same coupon at once.

When they got back inside, the teacher was busy giving out one of his daily presents—a test. He had no idea what was about to happen. Then all of a sudden his ears began buzzing. This time it was a *real* cataclysm. The kids were stamping their feet and shouting and whistling and drumming and banging, and some were even blowing horns. This was *not* music—this

was a rowdy uproar! Monsieur Noël realized that each and everyone of them had used the "coupon for making a lot of noise."

And just at that instant, Madame Incarnation Perez walked into Monsieur Noël's classroom. To add to the racket, she screeched out an ear-splitting, "Monsieur Noël, come to my office immediately!" But she said nothing to the students. After all, the students are the responsibility of their teacher.

Before leaving, Monsieur Noël begged for a coupon from Benedicte, because this time, even Hubert Noël was scared.

❧

Incarnation Perez was standing just behind her office door, cooking up a suitably humiliating treatment, when she saw a coupon being slipped under the door. She didn't want to bend down and pick it up, but her curiosity got the better of her. She heard footsteps disappearing as her prey walked down the hall, and when she looked down, she saw the words, "One coupon for getting out of trouble." Hubert Noël had had many trials in his life and faced them with dignity, but this time he plain chickened out.

Madame Perez hollered out loud, "He's not getting away with this!"

When he arrived back in class, the students had another surprise for him. They had set a chair in the middle of the room and were lining up in front of it. Charles promptly asked the teacher to sit down. Each student had a coupon ready. One by one, they handed their coupon to the teacher, and gave him a big fat kiss on both

of his chubby cheeks (as is done in France). A kiss to make him feel better, and to make themselves feel better. Nothing works like a kiss.

"Fifty-four kisses!" said Serge, who had been counting.

"Oh no, kisses are not for counting," said Santa.

No one noticed Incarnation Perez at the door. She crept away feeling a little sad. She too would have liked a kiss.

Over the next month, the war between the wicked principal and the gentle teacher was a silent one. Hubert Noël was the sheep avoiding her, and she was the lion waiting to attack her prey. Long before Valentine's Day, the kids had discovered that it was much more fun to use their coupons en masse, and that was why on

Valentine's Day Monsieur Noël found himself in front of an empty class, except for Charles who had already used his "One coupon for skipping a day of school." In fact, Charles had no coupons left. He had used them all up months earlier.

Monsieur Noël suggested a game of chess.

"I don't know how to play."

"That's why you come to school. I'll teach you."

Incarnation Perez was stalking around, spying, observing, watching, and waiting. Indignant, and somewhat jealous, she decided then and there to take action to get rid of Hubert Noël. He was near retirement age anyway, she thought, and his time had come. He was disobedient, disorderly, undisciplined, and *wild*. What's more, she hated his guts!

After lunch the teacher asked Charles to help him invent another set of coupons. He didn't tell him that he wanted to give them to Principal

Perez, but the coupons he suggested were in an altogether different category.

"One coupon for a smile," suggested Monsieur Noël.

Charles continued with:

One coupon for laughing

and

One coupon to tell a joke.

Together they made a list:

One coupon to do whatever you like
One coupon to have a party
One coupon to take a bubble bath
One coupon for sunbathing
One coupon to say, "Buzz off!"
One coupon to ask a tactless question
One coupon to have your own way
One coupon to have dinner with friends
One coupon to go on a picnic
One coupon for a day at the beach
One coupon to go hiking in the mountains
One coupon to make up a poem

One coupon for a spin on a merry-go-round
One coupon to go shoe shopping

Charles, whose grandmother would have liked the idea, wanted to add

One coupon to help mankind
One coupon to hug an old person
One coupon to visit people in the hospital

Charles and the teacher spent the afternoon making several copies of this set of coupons. Hubert Noël was so pleased with this new set that he kept one in his pocket. Before leaving school that afternoon, he took out the "coupon to do whatever you like." But then he stopped in his tracks, thought for a moment, and realized that, like "Don't worry!" or "Be happy!" this was one of those things that are easier to say than do. Then he decided to take himself out to a really good meal at his favorite restaurant, the

Couscous Royal. That was before Incarnation swooped down on him and took his appetite away.

"This is absolutely inexcusable. Twenty-six students from the same class all absent! I called their parents and they all told me the same thing, some ridiculous story about coupons and excused absence. Who is behind this?"

The teacher was about to speak, but she wouldn't let him get a word in.

"Your so-called teaching methods are pathetic. You are ruining these children's chances. You are destroying my school's reputation. I will no longer put up with this anarchy. I will not allow you to teach them to be like you!"

The teacher couldn't help smiling. But his smile had no effect on the principal, he noticed—though he would have liked to help mankind by thawing her out a little. In fact, he wanted to invite her to have couscous with

him. But instead of doing that, he simply pressed the set of coupons from his pocket into her hands and ran for his life.

In the end, he didn't go to the restaurant. He ate leftover spaghetti and fell asleep in front of the TV.

Life came to the rescue by giving him ideas.

"Today we're going to do something of the utmost importance. We're going to make a pact."

The kids were impressed.

"First of all, we'll go round the class, and each of you will tell me what you did last night."

Twenty-seven times the answer was the same: "I watched TV."

"Fine. Now you're going to write down what you watched, give a brief summary, and evaluate the program: good, average, or no good."

"What if we don't remember?" asked one voice.

"In that case, just try to remember if it was good."

He collected the papers and counted up the evaluations, which he wrote on the board.

2 GREAT
2 GOOD
4 NO GOOD
8 CAN'T REMEMBER
11 AVERAGE

"Personally, what I saw was so exciting that it put me to sleep. So, if most of you agree that what you saw was only average, wouldn't we be better off to do without it?"

The students didn't see what he was getting at.

"I want to propose a pact: Choose one evening a week when you won't watch TV. Deal?"

You would have thought that he had put a knife into poor Charles, who had the TV in his bedroom.

"But Monsieur, that's impossible."

"Couldn't we try?"

Everyone signed the pact except Charles.

Even though the year was winding down, the teacher didn't stop having good ideas. True enough, not all the ideas suited everyone—the TV pact for example. But everyone liked the unexpectedness of his more surprising inspirations. And everyone agreed that Hubert Noël was as dynamic as a teacher half his age, everyone that is except . . . Incarnation Perez!

One of Monsieur Noël's innovations was a sort of mailbox—the discussion box—where the kids could drop in suggestions they had for subjects to talk about during their weekly group meeting.

Every Friday one kid would pull out a piece of paper without looking at it. Today it was Benedicte. She unfolded the paper, and blushed to the roots of her hair. She couldn't manage to pronounce the words written on it. She coughed a little, cleared her throat, had a fit of giggles, but not a word came out. Mohammed came to the rescue, pulling the paper out of her hand and taking a look himself. But then he just stood there, open mouthed. The paper was passed from hand to hand round the class like a hot potato.

It finally ended up with Charles, who didn't have the slightest problem reading the words on the paper, and was obviously disgusted with the others. "Making love!"

More hushed giggles were heard around the room.

"What's the matter with you all?" asked the teacher.

"It's disgusting sir!" said Laurent.

"I don't see why, Laurent."

Just as Monsieur Noël declared to the kids, "None of you would be here if your parents hadn't made love!" the door opened. Charles couldn't hold back the two syllables that gushed out:

"Uh oh!"

Incarnation Perez's eyes were daggers. She yelled, "Monsieur Noël, follow me!" Too bad there was no such thing as a "coupon for not following the principal."

As soon as Monsieur Noël walked out the door, Charles proclaimed sadly, "This is the end of us!" Everyone added a gloomy prediction to the list.

Even Laurent said, "Monsieur Noël really is a good guy."

"We were lucky to have him as long as we did. We really did get a lot of presents," said Mohammed. Benedicte started to cry. The whole class looked like they were at a funeral.

The verdict came back quickly, much too quickly. Mrs. Perez gave the teacher the letter she had received that very morning. It was a letter agreeing to her request not to renew Monsieur Noël's contract, thus forcing him to finally retire.

Hubert Noël was devastated. He had known he was taking a big risk by changing schools, but he always used this tactic when an old school became too quiet and he got the old wanderlust—wanting to meet new kids and try out new environments. He had been eager to penetrate this particular school, which was known as "the dungeon," though he hadn't realized that Principal Perez was the dungeon master! After all, you had to try to help change things and make bad better. But Hubert Noël knew that eventually everything had to end. He was already past the normal age of retirement in France. Now he would just have to find a different way to help the world along.

He went back to his class with his head held high. Even if Incarnation Perez had beaten him, he was still master of his class until the last day of school.

When the kids learned what had happened, they soon realized what it meant: it meant that their Santa might have given out his last presents—at least to fifth-graders. All the parents were willing to fight for this teacher they had at first found so bizarre. But Monsieur Noël said, "Don't worry! We had a good year together and I'm happy about that. I don't want to go to war. Just write to me next year."

○○

The week before summer vacation, Monsieur Noël looked his class over, and asked, "Who do you think I admire most, those of you who used up their coupons, or those who saved them up in their schoolbags?"

Sylvie, who was proud of the stock she had built up through swaps and trading put her hand up.

"The ones who saved them, Monsieur."

"Why do you think that?"

"Because it shows we can save."

"You're completely wrong! If I gave you those coupons, it was so you could use them! Now it's too late!"

A silence fell over the class, in some cases a silence of regret.

"When you're born, you get a whole bunch

of coupons. Which coupons am I talking about?"

Charles, who was now the world expert on coupons shouted out, "The coupon for being alive!"

"Right!" said the teacher, "And what else?"

"The coupon for walking!" said Laurent.

"The coupon for speaking!" copied Sylvie.

"The coupon for learning to read!"

"The coupon for learning languages!"

Benedicte's row continued with coupons for learning history, geography, biology, and all the other ologies.

"The coupon for sports!" said Laurent.

"The coupon for love," added Benedicte dreamily.

"The coupon for happiness."

"The coupon for crying."

"The coupon for making decisions."

Charles couldn't help adding his contribution:

"The coupon for talking about making love."

"Yes, I think you understand now. When we are born, we get all these coupons, and we might as well use them! Don't you agree? Tomorrow we're going to have a birthday party for life and for all the coupons life has given us. I'll bring the cake."

Once again it was Charles who had the idea for a present for the teacher. But he wasn't sure it would work.

The next day was the last day of school, and not a drop of work was done. The class spent the whole day having a party. Santa offered his students one last gift: a blank exercise book on which he had written:

"One coupon for telling your life story."

Then Charles handed him a huge envelope.

In it were twenty-six *wild card* coupons.

"What are you going to do with them?" asked Monsieur Noël.

"We are going to give you a present!" said Charles.

The teacher looked and read what they had written on a big piece of paper in gold ink:

"One coupon for a happy and well-deserved retirement."

The teacher smiled warmly, and before kissing his students thank you and good-bye, he said, "You're right, there's a time for everything."

At the end of the day, he picked up his giant coupon and left the school without a word to Incarnation Perez, and headed straight for his favorite restaurant, the Couscous Royal.